Mission Statement

You are the hero of this mission.

Each section of this book is numbered. At the end of most sections, you will have to make a choice. The choice you make will take you to a different section of the book.

Some of your choices will help you to complete your mission successfully. But if you make the wrong choice, death may be the best you can hope for! Because even that is better than being UNDEAD and becoming a slave of the monsters you have sworn to destroy!

Dare you go up against a world of monsters?

All right, then.

Let's see what you've got...

Introduction

You are an agent of **G.H.O.S.T.** — Global Headquarters Opposing Supernatural Threats.

Our world is under constant attack from supernatural horrors that lurk in the shadows. It's your job to make sure they stay there.

You have studied all kinds of monsters, and know their habits and behaviour. You are an expert in disguise, able to move among monsters in human form as a spy. You are expert in all forms of martial arts. G.H.O.S.T. has supplied you with weapons, equipment and other assets that make you capable of destroying any supernatural creature.

G.H.O.S.T.

You are in the dining room, sipping orange juice and waiting for your breakfast. Your butler comes towards you carrying a covered silver dish. The dish is making bleeping noises.

Cranberry puts the dish on the table in front of you and whips off the cover. "Your phone, Agent."

"Thank you, Cranberry." You check the screen. You have an email from the Director General of G.H.O.S.T.

"I think she wants me to get a move on," you say.

To set off immediately for Beijing, go to 37.

To research zombies first, go to 25.

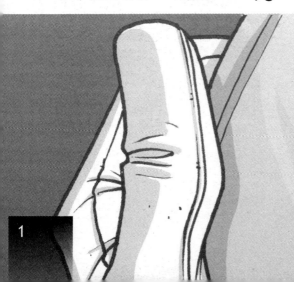

You are based at Arcane Hall, a spooky and secret-laden mansion. Your butler, Cranberry, is another G.H.O.S.T. agent who assists you in all your adventures, providing you with information and back-up.

Your life at Arcane Hall is comfortable and peaceful; but you know that at any moment, the G.H.O.S.T. High Command can order you into action in any part of the world...
Go to 1.

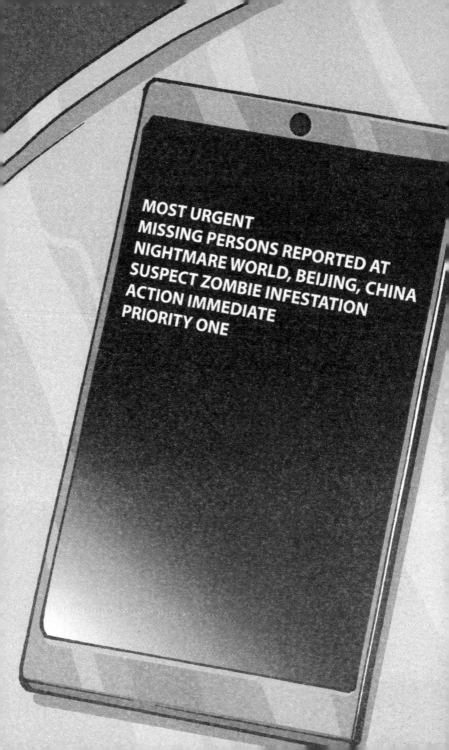

"I'll have to go the long way round," you tell Cranberry.

You sneak into the Snow White Mine Coaster unnoticed. The cars of the ride are like a train of mine carts, running on a track that heads into underground caverns and galleries.

You set the ride going and jump into the first cart as it moves off. As you do so, zombie dwarves appear at the mouths of shafts set into the walls and ceiling. They clutch at you as you pass. Several drop into carts behind you.

To use your flame pistol against the dwarves, go to 31.

To undo the coupling attaching your cart to the others in the train, go to 16.

3

You raise your flame pistol. "I'll burn her out," you tell Cranberry.

"ARE YOU MAD?" he shrieks. "You're in a roomful of hair — have you ever seen hair burn? You'll all go up like a torch!"

You quickly return the flame pistol to its sheath. "I knew that."

You reach for your dart gun.

Go to 22.

4

You draw your sword and flame pistol. You flip a grenade into the nearest group of zombies. As it explodes, you step forwards and carve a path through the undead creatures.

But you soon run out of ammunition, and your sword alone is not enough to keep the zombies at bay.

Go to 44.

5

The zombies press forwards. You try to fight them off with every weapon you have.

But you cannot use explosives inside the castle without bringing it down about your ears. You are soon out of ammo for your flame pistol and dart gun, and charge for your stunner. Eventually even your sword breaks. The zombies close in.

Go to 44.

6

"I'll pick it up from the airport," you say.

But when you touch down in Beijing, hours later, the truck has not arrived.

"It's caught in traffic," explains the Chinese officer sent to meet you. "People are fleeing the city. They're scared the zombies might break out. All roads are at a standstill."

"Then I'll have to go in without equipment," you say.

The Chinese have a military helicopter waiting. You board it, and soon you are over Nightmare World. The lights are off; all is dark below. "I'm going in," you say.

You abseil into the main square of the park. Too late, you hear shuffling noises in the darkness all around you.

Go to 44.

7

You fire the dart gun. Your aim is good, and the zombie collapses.

Unfortunately, it collapses onto the lever. With a clang, the points swing across, blocking the line.

The engine leaps from the track, throwing you clear. You slam into a tree and black out for a moment.

When you regain consciousness, you find to your horror that you are surrounded by zombies!

Go to 44.

8

You duck past the zombie Snow White, who is so busy munching she only makes a half-hearted attempt to stop you.

You burst back onto the mall. You are still some way from the drawbridge to the castle, with lots of zombies in between.

To fight your way through the zombies, go to 4.

To pretend to be one of them, go to 39.

9

You check your video and audio comms links that allow Cranberry, back at Arcane Manor, to see and hear everything you do. "Stay with me," you say, "I'm going in."

"Copy that."

You pull a large carry case from the truck, open it and start to assemble a hang-glider.

Half an hour later, the helicopter takes you up and releases you a couple of miles from the park.

You fly silently across the theme park without alerting the zombies. You touch down on the rooftop you have chosen as your landing place. You leave the glider and head cautiously for the Nightmare World control room.

Here, you throw the main switch to bring power back to the park. Lights flicker on. CCTV

screens stutter into life. Looking at them, you whistle softly.

"What is it?" asks Cranberry.

You stare at the screens showing the main concourse. "The zombies are having a costume parade," you say. "Maybe they remember that's what they used to do when they were alive. The gang's all there! Shambling Beauty, Slow Bite and the Severed Dwarves, Prince Chomping and Cinderipper, Little Dead Riding Hood..."

"Forget the sightseeing!" snaps Cranberry. "You have a job to do!"

At the same moment, zombies burst into the control room — they must have sensed your arrival after all!

To fight the zombies, go to 28.
To try and escape, go to 48.

10

You keep your back against the nearest wall and your eyes on the girl in the red cloak. "Are you okay?" you ask.

The girl looks up — and you realise where you've seen her before: at the costume parade. She's Little Dead Riding Hood!

The hooded zombie drops her basket of goodies and lunges towards you, thirsting for blood!

To use your stun gun, go to 29.
To use your dart gun, go to 38.

11

You tie Rapunzel's hair to the window frame
and start helping the family to climb down it,
allowing them to go first.

But the survivors are unfit and untrained.
They make a lot of noise, attracting zombies
to the foot of the tower.

The survivors reach the ground and run
into the shadows. You hear screams from the
darkness, and know they are survivors no longer.

By the time you reach the ground, you are
surrounded.

Go to 44.

12

"I think I've spotted two survivors," you tell
Cranberry. "A couple of kids. I'll try and get them
to safety."

You run after the children. As you catch up
with them, you realise that the boy is wearing
leather shorts and knee-socks, and the girl a
pinafore dress.

Those don't look like modern kids, you think.
They look more like Hansel and Gretel!

You skid to a halt. At the same moment, zombies step out from the trees, and Hansel and Gretel turn around. You realise that they like to eat more than gingerbread!

Go to 44.

13

"The theme park," you say.

You touch down at Beijing airport and are directed to a quiet corner where a helicopter is waiting, its rotors turning.

A Chinese officer steps forwards. "Please come with me."

The helicopter takes you swiftly to Nightmare World. It lands outside the park, where the Spook Truck is waiting. This G.H.O.S.T. vehicle contains a whole armoury of weapons and equipment.

You collect everything you need to destroy zombies: an electronic stun gun; a flame pistol; an air gun firing antiviral darts to kill the zombie virus; explosive grenades — and a samurai sword, in case all else fails!

You're ready to tackle the zombies. But how do you get into the park?

To abseil in from the helicopter, go to 21.
To talk to the Chinese army commander, go to 32.

14

You strain to turn the wheel that raises the bridge. But the mechanism is rusty and you are too slow. The bridge has hardly begun to move before the zombies arrive and lurch across it.

Go to 44.

15

You start down the stairs.

"What are you doing?" complains Cranberry. "Aren't you going to help those people?"

"I don't like heights," you tell him. "You're welcome to come out here and take my place!"

You reach the bottom of the stairs and rush out onto the mall — only to find yourself surrounded by zombies!

Go to 44.

16

You release the coupling, and the other cars fall behind. The dwarves they carry snarl and moan in frustration.

You slump down in the cart, and curse as you realise you are sitting on mining tools, including a pickaxe and a shovel.

Up ahead, more zombies are waiting on a ledge just above the track. You have to decide quickly how to deal with this new threat.

To use your flame pistol, go to 31.
To use the pick, go to 23.
To use the shovel, go to 42.

17

"Assemble a rescue squad," you tell the army commander. "I'll lead them in."

The park gates will have to be opened to let you into the park. Your plan is to rush them, destroying any zombies who get in the way.

But your plan misfires. As soon as the gates are opened, zombies surge out from Nightmare World, overwhelming your small force. Even as you fight bravely, you hear screams from the troops surrounding the park as they go down before the undead tide. You have unleashed the zombie apocalypse!

Go to 44.

18

You race up the stairs, pulling pikes and tapestries from the wall to clutter the route, holding the zombies up.

You find a door and burst out onto the battlements, where you see a group of terrified survivors.

Zombies pour through the open door behind you. The survivors scream in terror.

To fight to protect the survivors, go to 5.
To try and lead them to safety, go to 36.

19

The flame gun is drenched. You throw it away.

But before you can reach for another weapon, Cinderipper and Prince Chomping drag you back into their slipper! They plunge decayed teeth into your neck, one to each side.

Locked in a terrible embrace, you feel your consciousness slipping away. There is only one way to avoid becoming a slave to these rotten royals. You pull a pin on an explosive grenade. The blast kills the zombies and, mercifully, you.

Go back to 1.

20

With zombies in cold pursuit (which is like 'hot pursuit' only a lot slower), you head for the Slipper Ride. It looks like a log flume except that the 'logs' are Cinderella's glass slippers.

Zombies pour in through the entrance behind you. Quickly, you set the ride in motion and jump aboard the leading glass slipper. It carries you away, gathering speed.

"What am I floating on?" you ask Cranberry.

"Water."

"It's red," you tell him, "and it doesn't *smell* like water..."

The slipper tips. You look around to see two figures emerging from the back seats.

"Uh oh," you say. "It's Cinderipper and Prince Chomping. They were hiding back there. Yeuch! He's eating her face."

"Do you mean he's kissing her?"

You shudder. "No..."

The zombies start to climb over seats, heading towards you.

To fire your dart gun at zombie Prince Charming, go to 47.

To fire your flame pistol at the zombies, go to 41.

21

The helicopter hovers above the theme park's main square. The lights are off, but looking down you see lots of movement in the darkness below.

Curious, you abseil down. Too late, you realise that the noise of the helicopter has attracted a huge crowd of zombies!

You yell to the helicopter pilot to pull away. But it is too late! Zombies have already grabbed the trailing rope. Now they are pulling you down into their midst!

Go to 44.

22

You fire the dart into Rupunzombie's neck. She screams and her hair instantly grows back! She shambles towards you but then collapses. The antiviral drug has destroyed the virus that gave the creature its unlife.

"If you're right about the parade," says Cranberry, "she must be one of the park staff — the ones who dress up as characters. I guess they were the first to be infected."

"But how?"

"I'm still working on that..."

The family in the attic plead with you to help them escape.

To help the family get away from the tower, go to 11.

To tell them to stay put, go to 40.

23

As you approach the dwarves, you swing the pick.

The sharp point sticks in the chest of a dwarf and the handle is torn from your hands. You have lost your weapon! You are helpless as the other dwarves leap from the ledge into the cart, piling on top of you and starting to feed!

Go back to 1.

24

You take cover behind a closed-up souvenir stall. "I haven't found anything that could be the source of the virus," you tell Cranberry. "I need more information."

"Right," he says. "This just in — the centrepiece of Nightmare World is a castle the owners brought over here stone-by-stone from Bohemia, and rebuilt as Sleeping Beauty's Castle. It's said the last Baron of the castle had a plantation in the Caribbean, and after a visit there he died mysteriously..."

"Then he could have brought back something from the Caribbean containing the zombie virus...!"

"Exactly," says Cranberry. "I'm guessing some sort of chest or casket. Someone on the park staff must have opened it."

"So it's probably in the castle," you agree. You look along the mall stretching before you. "But I'll have to work my way through a whole heap of zombies to get there."

To head for the Castle, go to 4.
To head for the Mine Coaster, go to 2.

25

"I'll be in the library," you tell Cranberry.

He stares at you. "If you say so."

You are reading a leather-bound book, **Shambling With Zombies**, when the computer screen at your desk bursts into life. The Director General is calling you.

"Why are you still there?" she storms. "Quit stalling and get in the air. Cranberry can brief you as you go."

Feeling like an idiot, you quickly slam the book shut. "Yes, Chief."

Go to 37.

26

You swing the samurai sword.

"I didn't see!" cried Cranberry. "Did you cut him off?"

"Sure did," you say, wiping zombie goo off the sword.

The other zombies scramble over the seats of the carriages towards you. Soon, you are fighting them off with sword, stun gun and your bare hands.

No sooner have you despatched the last one than the train reaches a station.

Spotting two young children running towards the witch's cottage, you bring the train to a halt.

To follow the children, go to 12.
To head for Grandma's House, go to 43.

You drop a grenade and dive for cover. The explosion destroys the drawbridge — and the zombies who had started to cross it.

You call Cranberry. "What am I looking for?"

"There's a chest in old photographs of the castle that looks a likely bet. I'm sending a photo."

Your phone beeps. You check the screen.

"Copy that."

The castle is full of dust and cobwebs. Sleeping knights in armour and nobles of a king's court lie all around. A veiled figure lying on a

stone table in the centre of the hall begins to
move. The veil falls away, revealing a ghastly
decomposing face.

"If that's Sleeping Beauty," you tell Cranberry,
"she's not getting a kiss from me!"

The nobles and knights scramble to their feet
with a clicking of bones and creaking of armour,
and lurch towards you.

**To fight Shambling Beauty and her
zombies, go to 5.**

To run for the stairs, go to 18.

28

You fight the zombies, but you know you cannot use explosives in the tight space without killing or seriously injuring yourself. Your stun gun, flame gun, and antiviral darts take out some zombies and your samurai sword accounts for others, but more keep coming!

Go to 44.

29

The zombie is already too close for you to use your sword. It surges forwards to sink its decaying fangs into your throat...

But you have managed to draw your stun gun. You press it against the zombie's body and pull the trigger.

Dead Riding Hood shudders as the current surges through her body, breaking the control of the zombie virus. Its unlife force destroyed, the creature drops to the floor.

You leave the cottage and return to the train.

Go to 46.

You reach out, catch a support of the upper flume and swing yourself up to land in the empty slipper.

With shrieks of rage, Cinderipper and Prince Chomping try to follow, but they are too clumsy. They fall back behind their slipper — and the churning flume tears their horribly decayed bodies apart. With unearthly wails, they sink beneath the waves and you sit back with a sigh of relief.

Go to 46.

31

You draw your flame pistol and fire at the dwarves.

But the tunnels through which the ride runs are not made of real rock; they are plastic fakes, which catch fire. Soon the whole mine is ablaze and full of choking smoke.

Coughing and clutching your throat, you succumb to the deadly fumes.

Go back to 1.

32

The Chinese army commander briefs you on the situation.

"We have the threat contained for now," he tells you. "The zombies cannot break out — but my soldiers have no experience of such creatures. That is why we sent for you.

"All the men I have sent in have been attacked, and themselves turned into zombies. My troops are horrified at having to shoot their old comrades! Soon, they will refuse to obey orders.

"What's more, there are survivors still in the

park — stuck on rides or hidden in places the zombies cannot reach. They are terrified. There is no time to lose!"

You consult Cranberry. "At all costs, you must prevent a breakout," he says. "There are one point four billion Chinese out there — that's an awful lot of zombies!"

To lead a rescue squad into the park, go to 17.

To go in alone, go to 9.

33

You press the stun gun to the zombie's neck and pull the trigger.

Nothing happens. The electric charge has run out.

Slow Bite grabs you and lives up to her new nickname...

Go back to 1.

34

You race up the stairs until you reach a room at the top of the tower.

The room is almost filled with Rapunzel's golden hair; now she is a zombie, it has all fallen out. Rapunzombie is trying to reach a family of tourists trapped in the attic above her room. Terrified faces peer through a trapdoor in the ceiling.

The zombie spots you and swings around, reaching for you with claw-like hands.

To use your flame pistol, go to 3.
To use your dart gun, go to 22.

35

Knowing that you have zombies on your tail, you decide to try the Forest Railway. You set the ride moving and climb into the engine cab. The train gathers speed as the zombies reach the platform, but some manage to get aboard.

At the trackside, you see one zombie shambling towards the points lever.

Cranberry has spotted him too, via his video link. "He'll wreck the train!" he cries. "Cut him off!"

To use your dart gun against the zombie, go to 7.

To draw your samurai sword, go to 26.

36

You shepherd the survivors away from the zombies. As you cross a narrow bridge, you drop a grenade, blowing the zombies to smithereens and destroying the bridge.

Finding another door into the castle, you tell the survivors to stay put and go through it. You begin your search, running in and out of empty rooms while the noise of zombies grows louder.

At last, you find a furnished bedroom — and there is the chest you are looking for!

You open it. Inside lies a skull wearing a top hat and dark glasses.

"Baron Samedi!" gasps Cranberry.

"What?"

"He's a sort of top zombie spirit."

"There's a bottle of rum, too," you say. "What's the betting that's the source of the zombie virus?"

To destroy the bottle, go to 45.
To destroy the chest, go to 50.

A few minutes' drive takes you to your private airfield where your personal jet, the Phantom Flyer, is kept in constant readiness.

You are soon in the air. Over the North Sea, you speed up to supersonic flight.

You call Cranberry. "What have we got on Nightmare World?"

Cranberry's voice crackles in your headphones. "It's a theme park with lots of dark rides based on the Grimms' fairy tales."

You sniff. "Sounds kind of cutesy."

Cranberry sounds amused. "Have you read any of those stories? I mean the originals, before they got cleaned up for little kids?"

"Er, no."

"Then I think you're in for a shock."

You shrug. "Okay. Give me a refresher on zombies."

"What makes people into zombies is a virus. First it kills the humans it's infected and then it reanimates their bodies. It doesn't have as much control as the brain, so zombies are poorly co-ordinated — they don't see well, they can't speak and they shamble. They don't think — all they want to do is to feed and make more zombies. So when you destroy one, you are killing a virus, not a person. Wait one..." After a minute's pause, he continues, "Our Beijing agent wants to know where you want to pick up our Spook Truck."

To have the truck sent to Beijing airport, go to 6.

To have it sent to Nightmare World, go to 13.

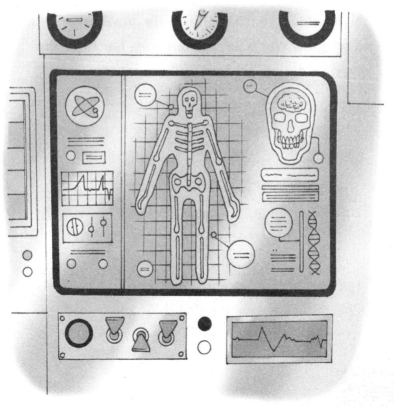

38

You draw your dart gun and fire. But the zombie turns her head and the dart buries itself in the cloth of her hood, failing to reach its target.

Before you can fire again, the door and both windows of the cottage are smashed and rampaging zombies pour in.

Go to 44.

39

You have just reached the castle drawbridge when Snow White lurches out from her ride. She gives a wordless screech and raises a decaying

arm to point at you. The zombies in the mall finally catch on and start to shamble towards you. You have to act fast!

To try to raise the drawbridge by hand, go to 14.

To blow up the drawbridge, go to 27.

40

You tell the family to stay where they are before tying Rapunzel's hair to the window frame and abseiling down it. Zombies on the ground spot you but are too slow to react. You escape them and find a temporary hiding place behind a dumpster.

"There are too many to fight," you tell Cranberry. "I can't take them all out before they get me."

"You may not have to," Cranberry tells you. "My research suggests there's probably a single source for the infection. Destroy that, and you destroy the zombies."

"Great! So what is it, and where do I find it?"

"Those are the bits I haven't worked out yet."

"So what's your advice?"

"Keep moving."

The dumpster shifts with a squeak and a rumble of wheels. The zombies have found you!

You break cover and find yourself between the entrances of two rides.

To take Cinderella's Slipper Ride, go to 20.

To take the Red Riding Hood Forest Railway, go to 35.

The slipper climbs a moving belt as you draw your flame pistol.

You raise the gun to fire — and the slipper plunges down a slope. You pull the trigger just as the slipper ploughs through a water-splash, drowning the flame. Losing your balance, you fall into the water.

As you break the surface, you find yourself approaching a crossing point where the flume passes over itself. Another slipper is approaching at the upper level. The zombie prince and princess reach out to pull you back into their slipper!

To fight the zombies, go to 19.

To jump into the other slipper, go to 30.

You swing the shovel, sweeping the dwarves from their ledge.

Shortly afterwards, the cart stops at the end of the ride. You step out. But at the same moment a shambling shape appears in the tunnel leading to the exit.

"It's the zombie Snow White," Cranberry tells you helpfully. "She's eating something — is that a poisoned apple?"

"No," you say slowly. "I'll give you a clue. We all have one inside us, it beats, and it's kind of apple-shaped..."

"Yeuch!" says Cranberry.

To fight Snow White with your stun gun, go to 33.

To try and run past her, go to 8.

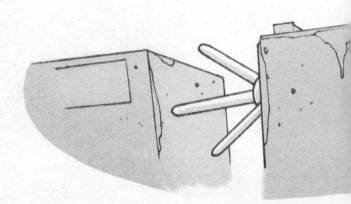

You head through the trees, watching for hidden zombies.

You reach a small cottage in a clearing. You hear moaning coming from inside. You ease the door open, draw your sword and creep through.

You are in a small room almost filled by an old-fashioned four-poster bed with curtains drawn. On the floor, a young girl in a hooded red cloak lies weeping.

As you step forwards, the curtains surrounding the bed are torn aside. A snarling zombie wearing a tattered nightgown over its wolf costume leaps at you. But you are ready, and swing your sword.

"Why, Grandma," you say, "what a short neck you have."

To help the girl on the floor, go to 49.
To keep your distance from her, go to 10.

44

The ravening zombies are upon you, tearing, biting and ripping at your flesh.

Your agony is brief. As consciousness slips away, your last thought is that you will now become a zombie yourself — a mindless slave of the creatures you sought to destroy!

The hunter has become the hunted! Go back to 1.

45

You reach for the bottle.

"Don't touch it!" warns Cranberry.

You try to snatch your hand back — but something seems to be drawing it onwards. In the struggle between mind and muscle, you knock the bottle over, splashing its contents over your hand.

Immediately, you feel the zombie virus infecting you. As it courses through your body, you know that this is what happened to the member of staff at the park who first found the bottle, and went on to infect all the others. But that knowledge will do you no good now...

Go back to 1.

46

You reach the end of the ride. As you disembark, you hear the shuffling sound of approaching zombies.

If you've come from the Red Riding Hood Railway, go to 20.

If you've come from the Cinderella Slipper Ride, go to 35.

If you've been on both, go to 24.

47

You draw your dart gun and fire at Prince Chomping. But the rocking of the slipper spoils your aim. The dart goes wide. Before you can fire again, the zombies are upon you! Just as they grab you, the slipper tips as it rounds a corner. The shock breaks the zombies' grip and throws you clear of the flume.

Dazed by the fall you look up — and realise to your horror that you are surrounded by zombies!

Go to 44.

You race for the fire escape and leap onto the next rooftop. The zombies are too badly co-ordinated to match your jump — those that try fall short and plummet to earth, hitting the ground with nasty squelching sounds.

You speed over the rooftops until you arrive at one of the park's main attractions. You look up at the dizzying height of Rapunzel's Tower of Terror.

Small figures are waving at you from the top of the tower. You hear their cries for help.

You use a grenade to blow a hole in the tower wall. Once inside, you find yourself on a landing with staircases going up and down.

To go down, go to 15.
To go up, go to 34.

49

You tap the girl on the shoulder. "You're safe, now..."

The girl looks up. Too late, you remember the zombie you saw in the parade earlier. The girl isn't Little Red Riding Hood any more — she's Little DEAD Riding Hood, and she wants more to eat than a basket of goodies...

Before you can react, she lunges forwards, sinking her teeth into your unprotected throat.

Go back to 1.

50

You draw your flame gun, aim it into the chest and pull the trigger. The bottle bursts and the rum inside erupts into flames, enveloping the skull. The air fills with savage, anguished screaming. You keep pulling the trigger until there is nothing in the chest but soot and ash.

You open the window and look out. All over the park, zombies are collapsing into ruin as their animating spirit is destroyed. The nightmare of Nightmare World is over.

"Tell the Chinese military to come in," you say

to Cranberry. "They can clear up and rescue the survivors. I'm heading back for breakfast — and this time I want bacon and eggs, not another mission!"

"Anything for a Hero," says Cranberry.

Phantom Flyer: For fast international and intercontinental travel, you use the Phantom Flyer, a supersonic business jet crammed full of detection and communication equipment and weaponry.

Spook Trucks: For more local travel you use one of G.H.O.S.T.'s fleet of Spook Trucks — heavily armed and armoured SUVs you requisition from local agents.

Electronic Stun Gun

Flame Pistol — zombies don't like fire!

Dart Gun — fires antiviral darts to kill the zombies

Explosive Grenades

Samurai Sword

MONSTER HUNTER

ALIEN

STEVE BARLOW ◇ STEVE SKIDMORE

Illustrated by PAUL DAVIDSON

You are an agent of **G.H.O.S.T.** — Global Headquarters Opposing Supernatural Threats.

Our world is under constant attack from supernatural horrors that lurk in the shadows. It's your job to make sure they stay there.

You are crouching in a dark cellar, hunting down a monster. You don't know what type of monster it is, but you have to deal with it before it deals with you!

You look at your MAAD — Monster And Alien Detector — on your wrist. It starts to flash red. There is an alien in the vicinity...

Continue the adventure in:

MONSTER HUNTER
ALIEN

About the 2Steves

"The 2Steves" are
Britain's most popular
writing double act
for young people,
specialising in comedy
and adventure. They
perform regularly in schools and libraries,
and at festivals, taking the power of words
and story to audiences of all ages.

Together they have written many books,
including the *I HERO Immortals* and *iHorror* series.

About the illustrator:
Paul Davidson

Paul Davidson is a British
illustrator and comic book artist.

I HERO Legends — collect them all!

ATHENA
978 1 4451 5234 9 pb
978 1 4451 5235 6 ebook

BEOWULF
978 1 4451 5225 7 pb
978 1 4451 5226 4 ebook

KING ARTHUR
978 1 4451 5231 8 pb
978 1 4451 5232 5 ebook

FREYA
978 1 4451 5237 0 pb
978 1 4451 5238 7 ebook

HERCULES
978 1 4451 5228 8 pb
978 1 4451 5229 5 ebook

ROBIN HOOD
978 1 4451 5183 0 pb
978 1 4451 5184 7 ebook

Have you read the I HERO Atlantis Quest mini series?

MENACE FROM THE DEEP
978 1 4451 2867 2 pb
978 1 4451 2868 9 ebook

OCEAN ALLIANCE
978 1 4451 2870 2 pb
978 1 4451 2871 9 ebook

BATTLE FOR THE SEAS
978 1 4451 2876 4 pb
978 1 4451 2877 1 ebook

ATLANTIS ASSAULT
978 1 4451 2873 3 pb
978 1 4451 2874 0 ebook

Also by the 2Steves...

978 1 4451 5104 5 pb
978 1 4451 5119 9 eBook

Immortals HERO
Ninja
Steve Barlow - Steve Skidmore

You are a skilled, stealthy ninja.
Your village has been attacked by a
warlord called Raiden. Now YOU must
go to his castle and stop him before
he destroys more lives.

978 1 4451 5101 4 pb
978 1 4451 5117 5 eBook

Immortals HERO
Warrior Princess
Steve Barlow - Steve Skidmore

You are the Warrior Princess.
Someone wants to steal the magical
ice diamonds from the Crystal
Caverns. YOU must discover who
it is and save your kingdom.

978 1 4451 5103 8 pb
978 1 4451 5121 2 eBook

Immortals HERO
Unicorn
Steve Barlow - Steve Skidmore

You are a magical unicorn.
Empress Yin Yang has stolen Carmine,
the red unicorn. Yin Yang wants to
destroy the colourful Rainbow Land.
YOU must stop her!

978 1 4451 5102 1 pb
978 1 4451 5124 3 eBook

Immortals HERO
Spy
Steve Barlow - Steve Skidmore

You are a spy, codenamed Scorpio.
Someone has taken control of secret
satellite laser weapons. YOU must find
out who is responsible and
stop their dastardly plans.